Looking For America's Dog

STEVEN WEISSMAN × FANTAG[...]

SECKRETARY OF STATE

~~I WAS CLEANING OUT MY DESK, I WAS EXPLORING A RUN FOR THE PRESIDENCY, & I WAS ACCEPTING AN AWARD FOR MY WORK IN 2012 ... SOME ASSHOLE COLD-COCKED ME & STOLE MY AWARD.~~ SO.. ALL PACKED ~~& SEE YEAH, I HAVE JUST 1~~ MORE ASSIGNMENT ~~AND THEN~~ BEFORE I'M FINISHED OH YEAH? WHAT'S UP? YOU'LL SEE, JOE ... YOU'LL SEE ~~COOL ... SO, THEN WHAT?~~

~~THAT'S COOL, MAN~~

INFO.
MOBILITY
DEFENSE

NATIONAL
BASKETBALL
ASSOCIATION

1

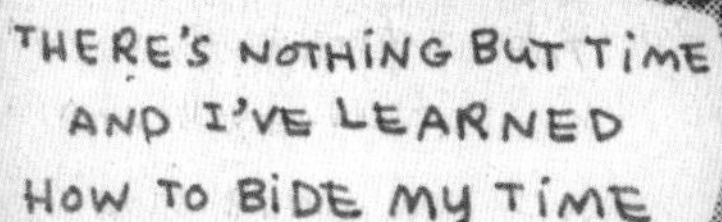

WASHINGTON, D.C.

BARACK HUSSEIN OBAMA
SASHA, HONEY, COULD I GET YOU TO LOOK INTO THE CAMERA?
NO
BUT, WHY NOT?
C'MON, SASH
I HAVE STUPID LOOKING EYES
WHO TOLD YOU THAT?
YOU HAVE BEAUTIFUL EYES!
THEY'RE HATE-FILLED HOLES

BARACK HUSSEIN OBAMA! WHAT THE FUCK IS GOING ON WITH THIS HOLIDAY CARD??
WUT?

LOOK! LOOK AT THAT SHADOW
TAP
ppy Holiday

IT JUST KEEPS DOING THAT!
TAP
TAP
ppy Holiday

IS THIS SUPPOSED TO BE FUNNY? WE'VE ALREADY MAILED THOUSANDS OF THESE!
Happy Holiday

HILLARY RODHAM CLINTON
I CANNOT BELIEVE YOU'VE RESIGNED YOUR POST..!
RELAX, JOE. YOU'RE NOT RID OF ME YET

OH? AM I GOING TO BE YOUR VICE-PRESIDENT, TOO?
I AM NOT RUNNING FOR PRESIDENT

I AM NOT RUNNING FOR PRESIDENT
I DON'T SOUND LIKE THAT!

I AM NOT RUNNIN
FOR PRESIDENT

LAURA INGALLS WILDER

IF I HAD SOME MILK, I WOULD HAVE POPCORN AND MILK

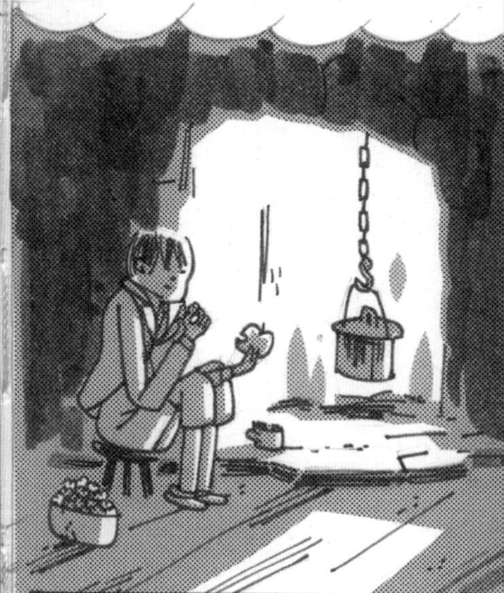

YOU CAN FILL A GLASS FULL TO THE BRIM WITH MILK, AND FILL ANOTHER GLASS OF THE SAME SIZE BRIM FULL OF POPCORN...

AND THEN YOU CAN PUT ALL THE POPCORN KERNEL BY KERNEL INTO THE MILK, AND THE MILK WILL NOT RUN OVER

YOU CANNOT DO THIS WITH BREAD. POPCORN AND MILK ARE THE ONLY TWO THINGS THAT WILL GO INTO THE SAME PLACE

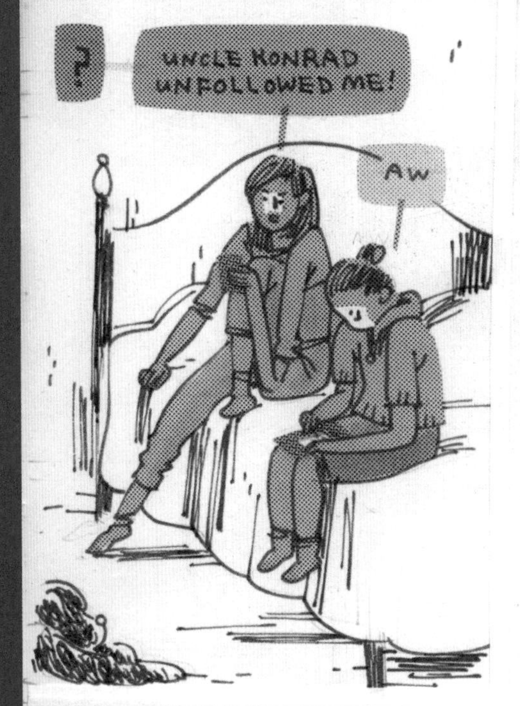
BARACK HUSSEIN OBAMA
?
UNCLE KONRAD UNFOLLOWED ME!
AW

I'M SURE HE WAS JUST CREEPED OUT BY HOW DESPERATE YOUR FEED IS
SHUT UP
IT'S TRUE

IT'S EITHER PICTURES OF YOU MAKING THAT SAME STUPID FACE YOU ALWAYS MAKE-OR- IT'S A SURVEILLANCE PHOTO OF THAT IDIOT BOY YOU'RE STALKING
I'M GOING TO KILL YOU NOW
WOULD YOU?

WHAT ARE YOU BUILDING, ANYWAY? IS THAT SUPPOSED TO BE A NATIVITY SCENE?
YES, IT IS CHRISTMAS, DUM-DUM

Merry Christmas

This year I'm returning all of your dead children to you

I know you want that more than anything

The End

SECRETARY OF STATE
ALL PACKED?
THERE WASN'T MUCH TO PACK

ALL I HAVE LEFT HERE IS PITY + ENVY
AND I WON'T NEED THOSE WHERE I'M GOING...

THAT'S COOL, MAN

I WON'T NEED THOSE WHERE I'M GOING
THAT'S COOL
HONK HONK!

NY-PRESBYTERIAN HOSPITAL

NOW, YOU MIGHT FEEL A WARM SENSATION...

IT'S NOTHING TO WORRY ABOUT

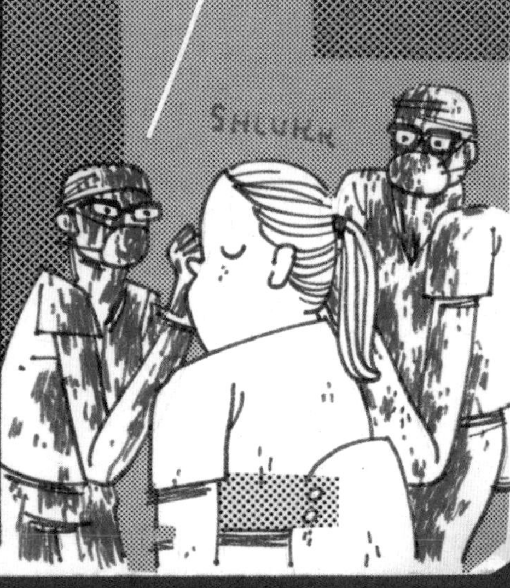

NEW YORK CITY

WASHINGTON, D.C.

BARACK HUSSEIN OBAMA

IT'S MY OWN STUPID FAULT FOR LEAVING JOE BIDEN IN CHARGE

BO!

HERE, BO!

BO!

IF I DON'T FIND THIS DOG BEFORE SCHOOL LETS OUT, THE GIRLS ARE GOING TO BE VERY UPSET...

BO-OH!!

HOLY SHIT: MICHELLE IS GOING TO FUCKING KILL ME

BO-OH

GOD DAMN YOU, JOE BIDEN

WE'RE GOING TO FIND HIM

LOOKING FOR AMERICA'S DOG

SHTS

IT'S NOT HIM

SECRETARY CLINTON
GOOD TO SEE YOU
IT'S JOHN KERRY
UH??
IT TAKES A LOT OF GLUE TO HOLD THIS SHIT TOGETHER

--NATASHA--

Ha ha

Have you seen Bo today?

I haven't seen Bo all week

GIRLS

Brb

YOU'RE BEING RUDE TO OUR DINNER GUEST

SORRY

SECRETARY KERRY..?

WHAT'S YOUR OPINION ON THE WEATHER BALLOON TORTURE MEMOS?

LOOKING FOR AMERICA'S DOG

HAVE YOU REALLY SEEN OUR DOG, SASH?
I CAN SEE HIM NOW

WHERE IS HE? WHAT'S HE DOING?
HE'S WALKING ALONGSIDE A COUNTRY ROAD
OH, GOD! PLEASE DON'T LET BO BE RUN OVER BY SOME HICK TRUCK

DON'T WORRY, HE'S ON A LEASH
A LEASH?? BO ISN'T A LEASH DOG!
WAIT, THERE'S MORE

I'M SO BURNED UP SOME DUMMY HICK PUT A LEASH ON MY DOG!
I'M LOSING IT

MRS. OBAMA, YOU RADIATE SUCH CONFIDENCE AND STYLE. WON'T YOU SHARE YOUR SECRETS?
THIS IS HOW I DO IT

FIRST, ALWAYS TUCK YOUR SHIRT INTO YOUR UNDERPANTS. IF IT'S COLD OUTSIDE, TUCK IN YOUR SWEATER, TOO

ALSO, YOU'LL NEED A GOOD MOISTURIZER. DON'T BE CHEAP ABOUT IT; YOU ONLY GET ONE FACE

HERE'S SOMETHING: IF ANYBODY TELLS YOU THEY DON'T LIKE WHAT YOU'RE DOING, KEEP DOING IT. DO IT ALL THE FUCKING TIME

JOHN WILKES KERRY
KERR-BEAR! HOW'S THAT REWRITE COMING ALONG?
YEAH, KERR-BEAR!

I'D PREFER YOU DIDN'T CALL ME KERR-BEAR. MY HIGH-SCHOOL GIRL-FRIEND CALLED ME KERR-BEAR

AWE-SOME! LET'S TALK ABOUT HIGH-SCHOOL FOR A WHILE

AWKWARD

17

POPES DON'T QUIT
STOP FILLING YOUR HEARTS WITH GARBAGE
DON'T BE SO GAY
SORRY, LADIES
POPES DON'T CRY

LOOKING FOR AMERICA'S DOG
I HAVE NEVER STOOD FACING THE OCEAN AND NOT FELT I WAS FACING EAST
I KNOW MANY GREAT AMERICANS WHO FEEL SIMILARLY ORIENTED TO THE SOUTHERN AND WESTERN HORIZONS...
BARACK HUSSEIN OBAMA GREW UP IN HAWAII AND INDONESIA. HE HAS NO SUCH FIXED ORIENTATION

LOOKING FOR AMERICA'S DOG

I KNOW WHERE
THE FLOOR GIVES WAY

I KNOW BENEATH
WHAT TERRORS LAY

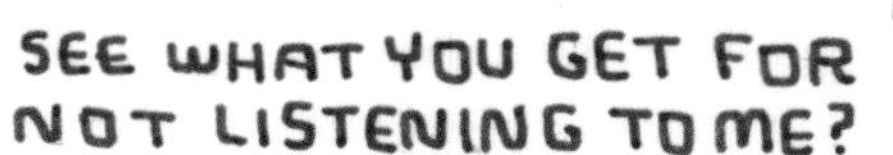
SEE WHAT YOU GET FOR NOT LISTENING TO ME?

SEE WHAT YOU GET FOR NOT TAKING ME SERIOUSLY?

THIS IS WHAT YOU GET

DZHOKHAR TSARNAEV

MY TONGUE'S SHOT OUT, MY LEG'S SHATTERED, BUT NOTHING CAN KILL THIS ENORMOUS BONER I HAVE

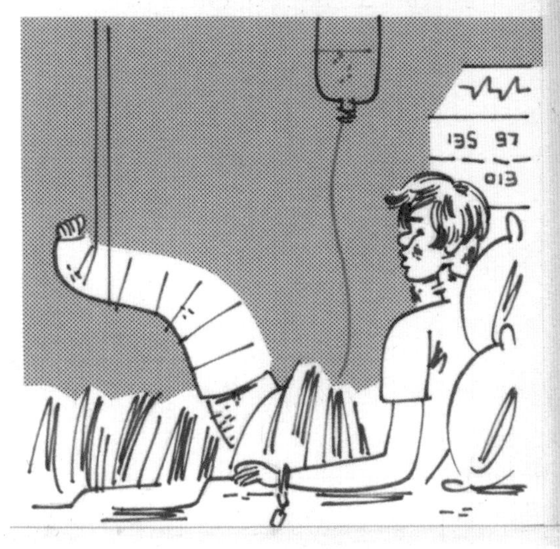

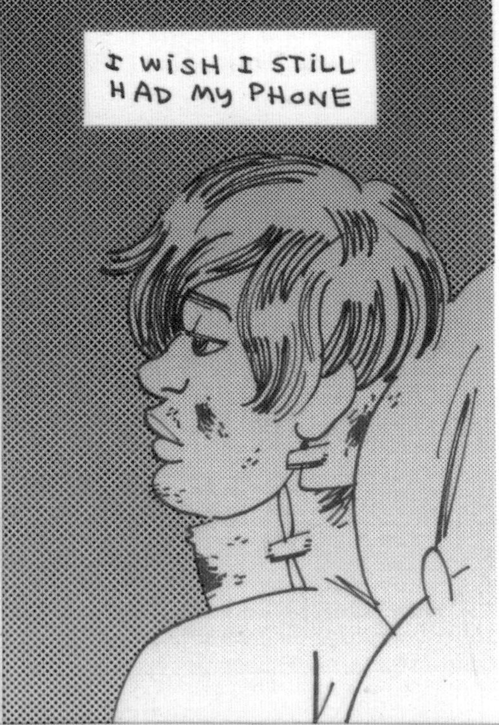

IT'S HARD TO BELIEVE THAT TAMER IS REALLY DEAD. I KEEP EXPECTING HIM TO WALK THROUGH THE DOOR

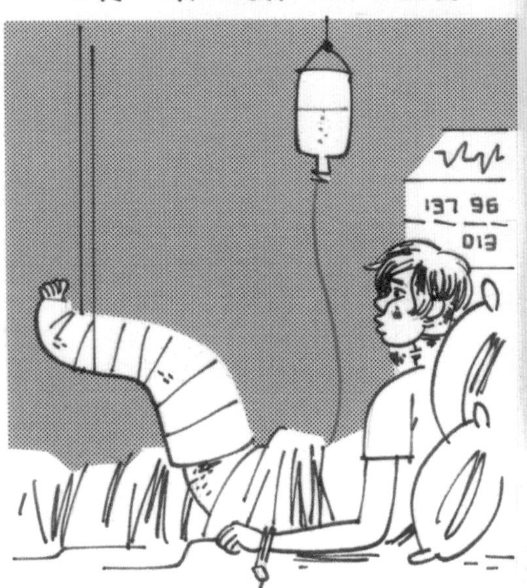

BARACK HUSSEIN OBAMA

MARTHA STEWART, THANKS FOR DROPPING BY

DONALD TRUMP, ARE YOU A TOM WAITS FAN, TOO??

I WANNA MARRY A LIGHTHOUSE

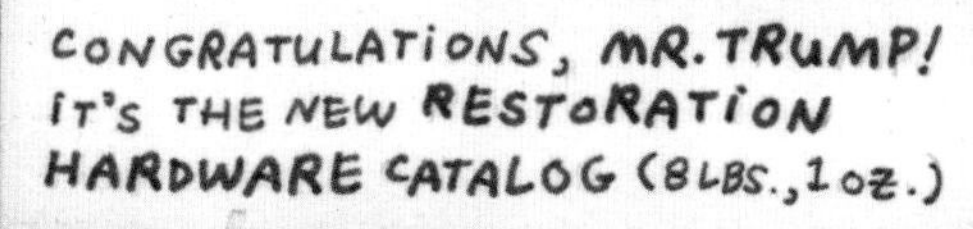

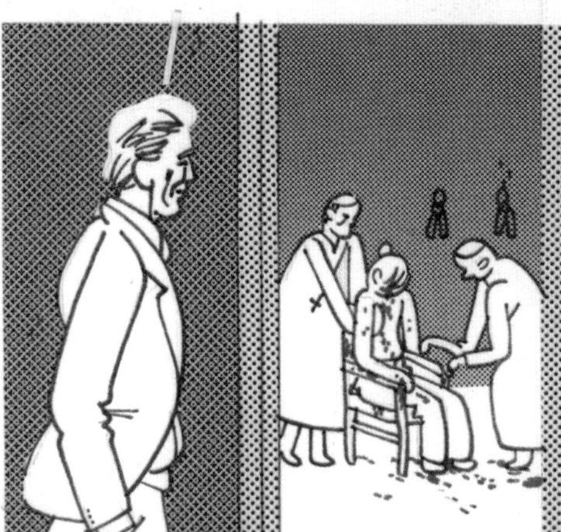
JOHN WILKES KERRY
MY JOB MAINLY CONSISTS OF CLEANING UP OTHER PEOPLE'S MESSES

THAT'S MOST JOBS

I'M SURE SOMEBODY CLEANS UP AFTER YOU

SOMEBODY WILL CERTAINLY BE CLEANING UP AFTER US

ROME

THEIR BREASTS ARE FULL OF MILK, AND THEIR BONES ARE MOISTENED WITH MARROW

THEY SPEND THEIR DAYS IN WEALTH, AND IN A MOMENT GO DOWN TO THE GRAVE

DON'T YOU REMEMBER? WE HATED THEM SO HARD

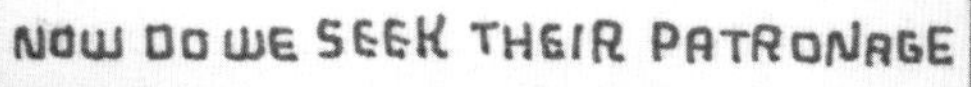
NOW DO WE SEEK THEIR PATRONAGE

BARACK HUSSEIN OBAMA

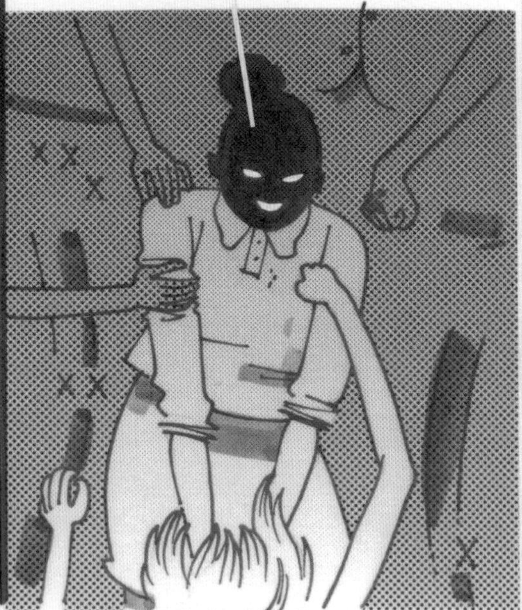

BARACK HUSSEIN OBAMA

NOW, AS LONG AS WE'RE ON THE SUBJECT OF DRONES, I'D LIKE TO CONGRATULATE SECRETARY KERRY ON HIS SUCC…SFUL WORK OVERSEAS …MIRITE?

MAM
MAM, PLEASE, LET ME FINISH

WE SWEAR BY ALMIGHTY ALLAH...

WE WILL NEVER STOP FIGHTING

YOU PEOPLE WILL NEVER BE SAFE

REMOVE YOUR GOVERNMENTS. THEY DON'T CARE ABOUT YOU

Natasha

THIS IS EARTH, NATASHA, IN THE YEAR 2113 OR SOMETHING
DON'T BE SCARED
OH, I SHIT

THERE'S A DINOSAUR CARVED ONTO MT. RUSHMORE NOW...
YOU DON'T SAY...

LET'S HIDE BEHIND THE LIBERTY BELL, THOSE UINTATHERIUM CAN BE NASTY
YAWNS

AND HERE IN GRANT'S TOMB IS YOU IN 100 YEARS! PERHAPS WE CAN LEARN HOW TO AVERT THIS CATASTROPHE
I SURE DIDN'T NEED TO SEE THIS

I'M SET TO BLOW YOUR MIND, SMART-ASS, BECAUSE THIS IS NOT 2113 OR SOMETHING
OH, NO
IT'S 2016
PSCHHX
I'M 14

G. KNIGHT WEISSMAN

AFTER EARTH II
THOSE ZEEBREX LOOK LIKE THEY WON'T GIVE US TOO MUCH TROUBLE
GOOD, I'M STARVING
YE-AH BITCHEZ!
YEE-AH!!
I'VE CAUGHT ONE, SASH! COME SLIT ITS THROAT
YE-AH
OH, SHIT! THOSE BARYLAMBDA ARE AFTER OUR LUNCH
LEMME GET JUST ONE BITE!
SONOFABITCH! THEY AREN'T EATING THE ZEEBREX AT ALL
THEY'RE TREATING HIS WOUNDS
THIS IS BULLSHIT!
MORE PRESSURE
SHHH

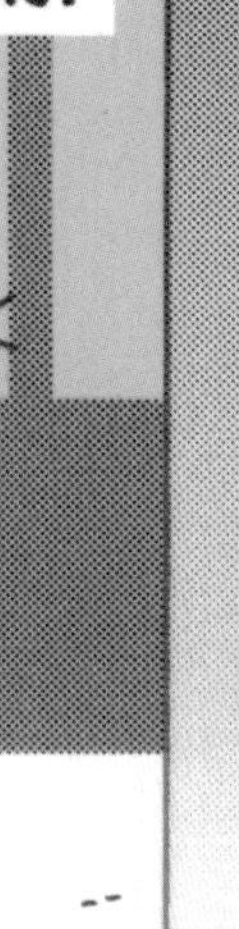

ANDREWS AIR FORCE BASE

* DAMASCUS *

I HAD NO IDEA THIS PLACE WAS SO COOL
ME NEITHER

EXCUSEME, WHAT ARE THOSE GUYS UP TO?
THAT SOLDIER IS BEING TREATED FOR EXPOSURE TO SARIN GAS

ALHAMMAM TAILORING
DO YOU THINK I'LL LOOK RIDICULOUS IN 14" CUFFS?
I THINK THEY'LL LOOK GREAT ON YOU BUT NOT VERY STATESMANLIKE
OH, SHIT
SPEAKING OF...
NO, WE HAVEN'T HEARD BACK FROM ~~~HEY!~~~ CAREFUL, THERE
I BEG YOUR PARDON
YOU HAVE A VERY LARGE PENIS

LOOKING FOR AMERICA'S DOG
SASHA, IS IT TRUE THAT YOU HAVE MAGIC POWERS?
NO
YOU LIAR
THEY'RE NOT MAGIC
THEY'RE JUST POWERS
TELL ME WHAT
NO
NO MORE CHRIS BROWN
I CAN'T TAKE IT
I WASN'T GOING TO SAY
LOOKN
GOOD
AURGH!!
CHRIS BROWN!

LOOKING FOR U AMERICA'S DOG

AMERICA'S DOG WENT TRICK OR TREATING WITH SOME 7TH GRADERS

THEY DIDN'T WEAR COSTUMES BUT NO ONE HAD THE NERVE TO REFUSE THEM CANDY

THE KIDS DROPPED ACID IN THE PARK AND ONE BOY TRIED TO STICK HIS KNIFE INTO ME

LOOKING FOR AMERICA'S DOG

AMERICA'S DOG WATCHES THE BOY CRY + CONVULSE IN THE UNDERGROWTH

THE BOY NO LONGER REMEMBERS THE LSD HE TOOK ONLY 3 HOURS EARLIER, AND DOESN'T KNOW WHY HE CAN'T ORIENT HIMSELF

AMERICA'S DOG COULD LEAD THE BOY TO THE COMFORT OF HIS FRIENDS IF HE WANTED TO

IT'S ENOUGH TO WATCH HIM SUFFER

LOOKING FOR AMERICA'S DOG

AROUND MIDNIGHT, AMERICA'S DOG ROUSED THE OCCUPANTS OF A NEARBY CABIN; A RETIRED COUPLE.

THE OLD MAN FOLLOWED AMERICA'S DOG INTO THE WOODS, WHERE THE DRUGGED BOY HAD FALLEN ASLEEP

WHEN THE BOY AWOKE, HE MISTOOK THE OLD MAN FOR HIS OWN GRAND-FATHER, WHO'D DIED WHEN HE WAS ONLY SEVEN

THE OLD MAN BROUGHT THE BOY HOME AND HIS WIFE FIXED HIM SOMETHING TO EAT

BARACK HUSSEIN OBAMA

I WAS THREE WHEN MY MOTHER TOOK ME TO IRELAND

I REMEMBER EATING BRAZIL NUTS ON THE DECK OF THE SHIP

EVERYONE ABOARD WAS PRETTY NERVOUS, AS THE TITANIC HAD SUNK THE PREVIOUS SPRING

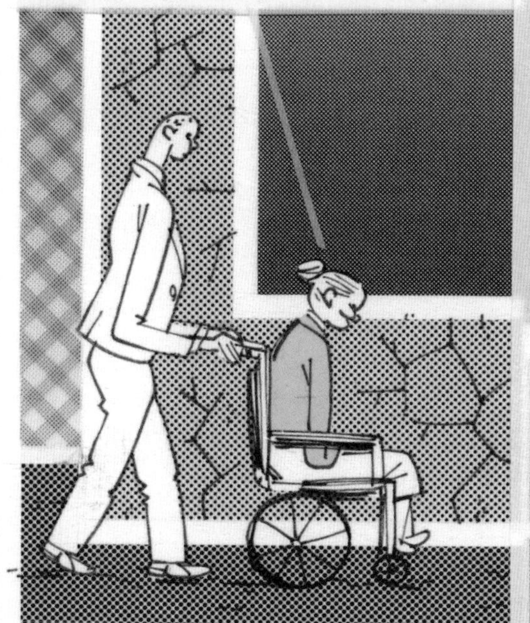

WHEN WAS THE LAST TIME YOU CHECKED ON THESE BIRDS?
IS THIS SUNDAY?

WASHINGTON, D.C.

TELL ME WHAT YOU SEE, NATASHA
HURRY BUDDY
I'VE GOT TO GET THIS TO MY BROTHER
HE'S VERY SICK!
I COULDN'T HELP HIM BEFORE BECAUSE I'M TOO FUCKED UP
BUT NOW
GIMME A MINUTE
STAND WATCH BUDDY
CHOF CHOF CHOF

THIS ALREADY HAPPENED

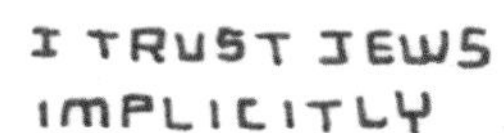
THIS IS HOW I DO IT

I TRUST JEWS IMPLICITLY

WHEN YOU CAN'T SQUEEZE ANYMORE TOOTHPASTE OUT OF THE TUBE...

Crest

CUT OFF THE BOTTOM AND SCRAPE IT OUT FOR THE NEXT BUNCH OF DAYS

Cres
DON'T EVER FORGET THAT YOU CAME FROM NOTHING

AND, EVEN IF YOU DIDN'T, YOU'LL SOMEDAY AMOUNT TO NOTHING

WASHINGTON, D.C.

LOOKING FOR AMERICA'S DOG

AMERICA'S DOG HAS BEEN LOCKED UP IN THIS CAGE FOR A WEEK WITHOUT FOOD OR WATER

HE ISN'T LONELY, THOUGH; THERE MUST BE 100 DOGS IN HERE

100 STARVING DOGS HOWL TOGETHER AS ONE

THE BLOOD OF OUR NATION'S ENEMIES IS WARM AND SWEET ON A COLD, WINTER MORNING.

I'M THE MOST HORRIBLE
AMERICA'S DOG HAS BEEN BROUGHT BEFORE THE SUPREME LEADER...
STOP CALLING HIM THAT!

NOW THE LEADER IS GIVING OUR DOG A MEDAL!
A MEDAL! WHAT FOR?

OMG

WHAT! WHAT IS IT, SASH?

WE'VE LOST HIM, MAL!

AMERICA'S DOG SITS AT THE RIGHT HAND OF THE SUPREME LEADER

ON THE LAST DAY OF EACH MONTH, THE LEADER ADJUDICATES DISPUTES BETWEEN ORDINARY CITIZENS

THE COMPLAINTS AREN'T REAL - MOST COMPLAINANTS HAVE NEVER MET BEFORE THEIR HEARING - NOT THAT IT MATTERS: THE LEADER'S JUDGEMENT IS ALWAYS THE SAME

TOSS THEM OUT OF THE WINDOW

ON A SNOWBOUND MORNING
IN ICY FOG
A GIRL IS WALKING WITH HER DOG

A RABBIT WAKENS + QUITS ITS BED
THE GIRL IS CRYING
HER DOG RUNS AHEAD

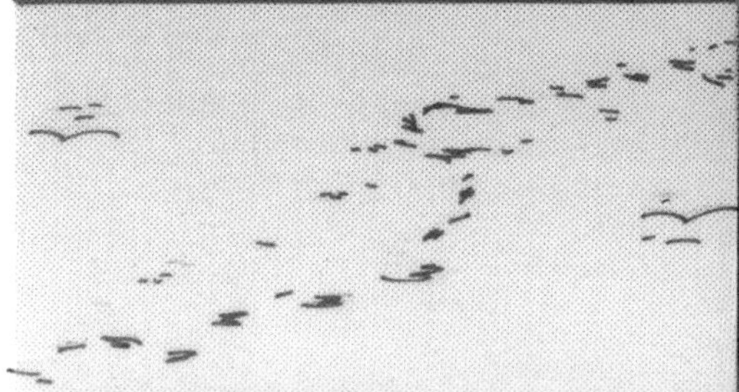
HER PLEAS ARE MUTED
HIS BARKING GROWS DIM
A SHOTGUN BLASTING SILENCES THEM

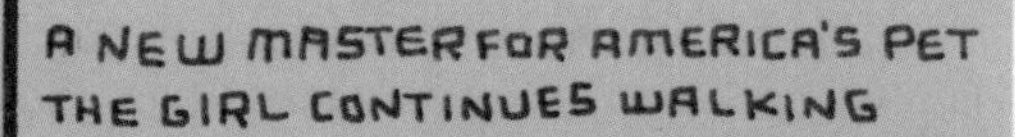
A NEW MASTER FOR AMERICA'S PET
THE GIRL CONTINUES WALKING

UNMET

DENNIS RODMAN, WE NEED YOU BACK IN PYONGYANG
AW, SHIT

WASHINGTON, D.C.

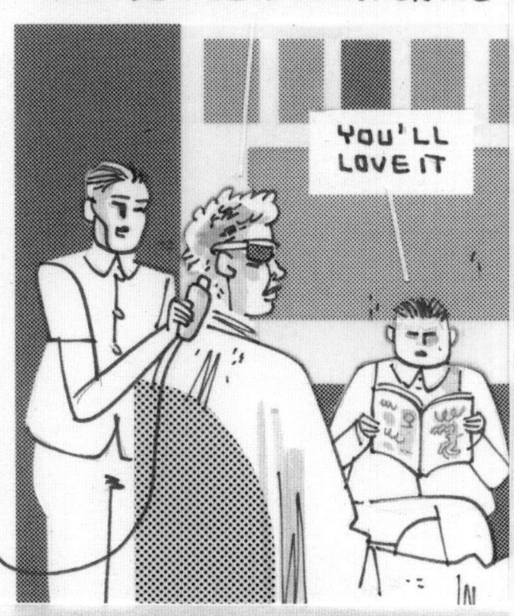
PYONGYANG BARBERSHOP
KIM, I REALLY DON'T THINK THIS WILL BE A GOOD LOOK FOR ME
YOU'LL LOVE IT

YOU KNOW MY NATURAL'S NEVER GOING TO LAY LIKE HIS, DON'T YOU?
그것은 완료

WHAT, ALREADY? BUT, I DON'T LOOK LIKE...
I LOOK LIKE...

FATHER!

LOOKING FOR AMERICA'S DOG

FATHER, YOU NEVER HAD TIME TO PLAY HORSE WITH ME WHEN YOU WERE SUPREME LEADER
JUMP SHOT
I'M SORRY ABOUT IT...

ALL DAY, BABY
NICE!
PMF!
CLAP
CLAP
ALL DAY!

DID I EVER TELL YOU ABOUT THE DOG I HAD GROWING UP? YOU KNOW, I ALWAYS WANTED TO BUY YOU A DOG...
I HAVE A DOG
YOU DON'T SAY

I DO. WOULD YOU LIKE ME TO FEED YOU TO HIM?
TAKE THE SHOT, WORM

THE WORM IS IN THE APPLE
FATHER, THIS IS MY DOG

WELL, HELLO THERE - UH - WHAT IS YOUR DOG'S NAME?

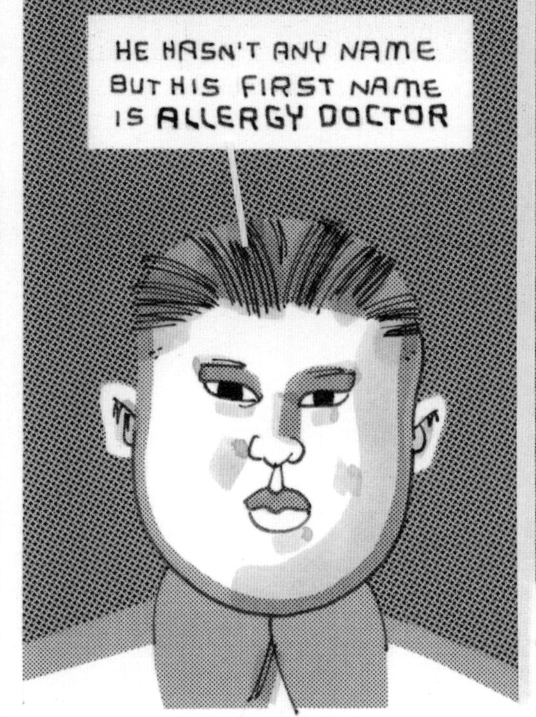
HE HASN'T ANY NAME BUT HIS FIRST NAME IS ALLERGY DOCTOR

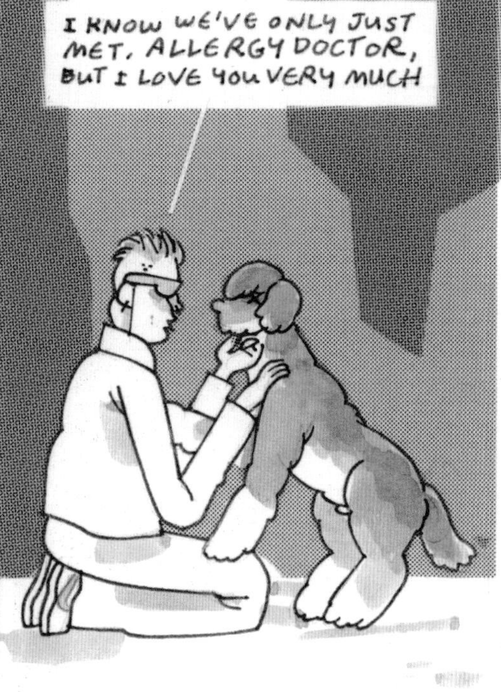
I KNOW WE'VE ONLY JUST MET, ALLERGY DOCTOR, BUT I LOVE YOU VERY MUCH

LOOKING FOR AMERICA'S DOG

THE FIRST TIME I EVER SAW A COYOTE WAS ON A NIGHT SUCH AS THIS

MAN, SUMMER NIGHTS IN TEXAS ARE A BITCH

I WAS WALKING MY OWN DOG THEN... I THOUGHT THE **COYOTE** WAS A DOG, TOO–**AT FIRST**–BUT IT DRIFTED ALONG SO STRANGELY, I BECAME CONVINCED IT WAS THE **GHOST** OF A DOG...

YOU KNOW, THE FIRST TIME I EVER SAW A SEAL, I THOUGHT THAT WAS **ALSO** A DOG! ONLY THIS DOG SEEMED TO BE DROWNING... I CALLED TO IT FROM THE **BEACH**, BUT IT WOULDN'T COME AND **I** COULDN'T **SWIM**...

WHAT ARE YOU DOING OUT HERE WITH MY DOG?
WOO
OOOH

RODMAN, HOW I USED TO ADMIRE YOUR DEFENSIVE PROWESS AND OFF-COURT OUTRAGEOUSNESS

I REALLY THOUGHT I WOULD LOVE YOU, AND MICHAEL, AND SCOTTIE...

FOREVER

THEN I GREW UP, AND YOU NO LONGER CONTRIBUTED TO MY HAPPINESS

THAT'S WHEN I REALIZED I DIDN'T OWE YOU A LIFETIME OF AFFECTION FOR THREE SEASONS OF CHAMPIONSHIP BASKETBALL...

ALLERGY DOCTOR

WHEN I SAW DENNIS RODMAN WALKING YOU OFF GROUNDS THE OTHER NIGHT, I WANTED TO KILL HIM THEN AND THERE
I'LL KILL ANYONE WHO TRIES TO TAKE YOU FROM ME, ALLERGY DOCTOR
?
WHAT THE FUSS?
WUF WUF
PAT PAT

HA
THERE'S A DOG LOOSE IN THE COURTYARD
KINDA LOOKS LIKE YOU...
THAT GUY LOOKS LIKE

ALLERGY DOCTOR!

LOOKING FOR AMERICA'S DOG

OH, MY ACHING BONES
LAST TIME I FELT THIS BAD, KARL MALONE WAS LAYING ATOP ME...
NOW, HOLD UP, BO;
I KNOW WHAT YOU'RE THINKING

HM
COME TO THINK ON IT, NOBODY'S QUESTIONED MY SEXUALITY IN A LONG OLD TIME...
I USED TO GET THAT SHIT ON THE REG

I GUESS, AT SOME POINT, PEOPLE DON'T LIKE TO THINK ABOUT YOU IN THAT CONTEXT ANYMORE
BIG MISTAKE, PEOPLE

DENNIS RODMAN IS SEXUALLY DANGEROUS
OHH
NOO

CARMEN ELECTRA

MADONNA

DEMI MOORE

Sunny
LOOK
DOGGY
DOGGY

NO

"DOG"

HARD CHOICES

IT FEELS LIKE THERE'S A HONEYBAKED HAM STUFFED UP MY ASS
YOU LOOK BEAUTIFUL

BABY SUBMARINE

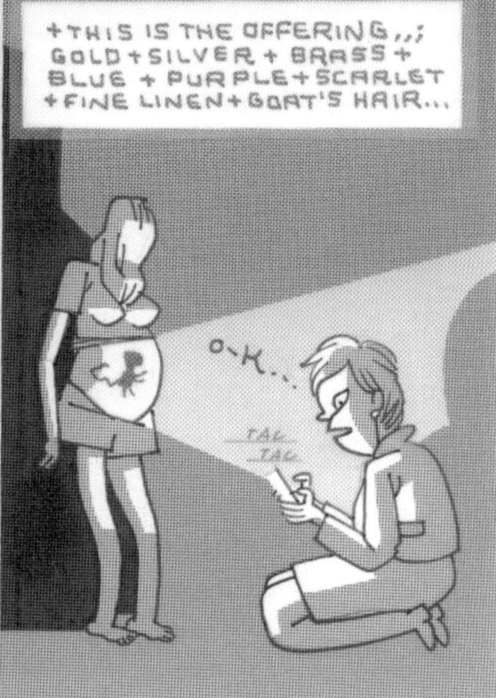

CHILDREN OF ISRAEL

LET THEM MAKE ME A SANCTUARY; THAT I MAY DWELL AMONG THEM

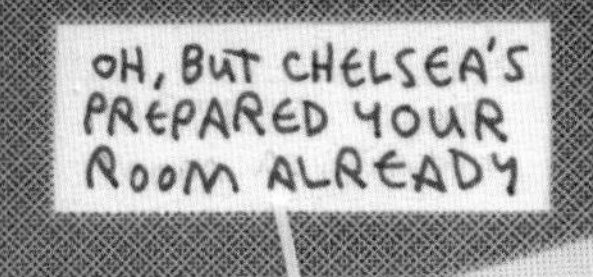
OH, BUT CHELSEA'S PREPARED YOUR ROOM ALREADY

TAC TAC

IT'S VERY NICE...
I THINK YOU WILL LIKE IT
COME + SEE

FANCY WALLPAPER, THE RODHAM FAMILY CRADLE, THERE'S EVEN A ROCKING HORSE...

WHAT DO YOU SAY TO THAT?

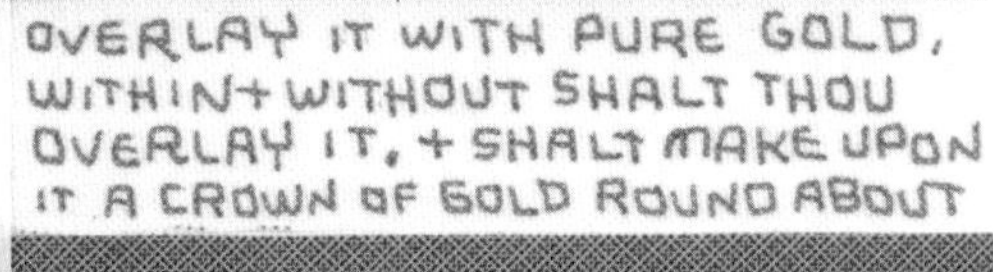
OVERLAY IT WITH PURE GOLD, WITHIN + WITHOUT SHALT THOU OVERLAY IT, + SHALT MAKE UPON IT A CROWN OF GOLD ROUND ABOUT

FUCKIN' RICH KIDS..!

Beach Day
?
WHY, HELLO, LADYBUG

OH! YOU'VE BROUGHT FRIENDS, HAVE YOU?
HA
HA

YUCK! WHAT'S WITH ALL THESE BUGS?
JESUS!

THEY'RE MAGICAL
YOU DUMB SHITS

STEVE

OBAMA SISTERS

SASH, IT'S 6AM, WE DON'T HAVE TO GET UP FOR ANOTHER 40 MINUTES...

HOW CAN YOU SLEEP, MAL?

CAN'T YOU HEAR THAT DOG?

I CAN'T HEAR ANYTHING

IT'S BEEN WAKING ME UP EVERY MORNING FOR LIKE A MONTH

DO YOU THINK IT'S BO?

I DON'T KNOW... I CAN'T REMEMBER WHAT BO SOUNDS LIKE ANYMORE...

I CAN'T HEAR ANYTHING
XXXXXXX XXX XXXX
ME NEITHER... THE BARKING'S STOPPED...

WASHINGTON, D.C.

Rats

MALIA, PLEASE SEND IN A.G. HOLDER...
RIGHT-O

WHAT DO YOU THINK, MAN? SHOULD I GO WITH THE DOUBLE MONK-STRAPS OR NORWEGIAN FRONT BLUCHERS?
??
LOOK DOWN

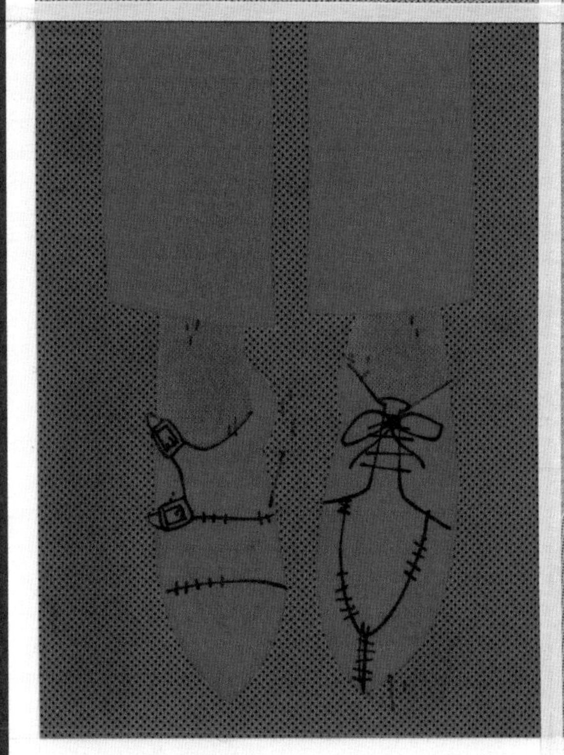

???
YOU CAN GO NOW

POLO

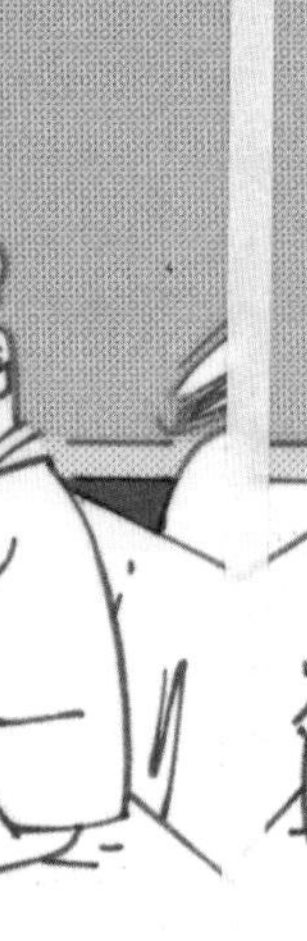

JOHN, HOW OLD WERE YOU WHEN YOU BEGAN TO WEAR COLOGNE?
FIFTY
FIFTY! DAMN
I'VE NEVER BEEN A COLOGNE GUY...
YOU SMELL LIKE PEE, JOE...
OLD MEN DRIBBLE
IT'S A FACT

JESUS! IS THAT WHY NOBODY TOUCHES ME?
YOU KNOW, JILL IS ASKING FOR A DIVORCE

YOU'RE GIVING OFF SERIOUS "HORNY HOBO" VIBES LATELY
YEAH, IT'S PRETTY GROSS
BLUBB

CHARLOTTE CLINTON MEZVINSKY
YOUR BABY IS SO CUTE!
IT'S SWEET OF YOU TO SAY SO...
I KNOW SHE LOOKS GROSS RIGHT NOW

DID YOU SEE MY PARENTS? ARE THEY STILL OUTSIDE?
YEAH
THEY LOOK HAPPY
THEY'RE PATHETIC

THEIR WORLDS HAVE NARROWED. FOR THEM NOW THERE IS ONLY FIGHTING AND KILLING AND STORING UP FOR WINTER...

THEY'LL NEVER HAVE ANOTHER BABY
YEAH!
FUCK THOSE GUYS

GHOST PRESIDENT
BEING A GHOST TAKES A LOT OF THE WONDER OUT OF EXISTING

FOR ONE THING, I CERTAINLY DON'T WONDER ABOUT GHOSTS ANYMORE

WHEN I TOUCH PEOPLE, THEY THINK IT'S JUST A DRAFT. BUT THAT'S HOW I KNOW I HAVE MASS: I CAN PUSH AIR AROUND.

SOMETIMES AIR PUSHES ME AROUND AND I CAN'T HOLD MY SHAPE. SOMETIMES PEOPLE BREATHE OR SWALLOW ME...
...IT GIVES THEM THE CREEPS

COMPUTERS

GIVE US CANDY

HEY DAD: CAN I HAVE SOME $ FOR MY HALLOWEEN COSTUME?

HALLOWEEN COSTUME?

YEAH! I'M GOING AS A SEXY DALEK

HERE'S MY SCHEMATIC

COSTUME

Big Bra

Extra Boobs

Tire

LOOKS GOOD TO ME

!?

YOU JUST SENT $10 TO MY STARBUCKS CARD?

WHERE IS KIM JONG UN?
Everyone in #NorthKorea say something mean to @HillaryClinton
HEH HEH

Notifications 10M+
?
CLICK

MEAN KOREAN TWEETS
SCROLL

Notifications 1
UH-OH

DEADLINE
WASHINGTON
MALIA, DID WE GET THAT FILE FROM KERR-BEAR YET?
NOPE!

OK, FUCK THAT GUY. HOW ABOUT JOE?
UM...
HE CALLED YOU A "DUMMY" ON TWITTER AND GOT 9 THOUS. RETWEETS...

OK, FUCK BOTH THOSE GUYS
DAD, YOU HAVE A MESSAGE HERE FROM A.G. HOLDER

THAT DUMMY? WHAT DOES HE SAY?
HE SAYS "FUCK YOU 4-EVER"

TIME

WHY IS FATHER SO UPSET?

HE DIDN'T WIN "PERSON OF THE YEAR"

HOO

Marian Shields Robinson

WHEN I LOOK AT YOU, I ONLY SEE YOU AS YOU ONCE WERE

YES, MOTHER ROBINSON...

WHEN I LOOK AT YOU TWO, I ONLY SEE YOU AS YOU WILL BE
YES, MEE-MAW

WHAT ABOUT ME, MOM? WHAT DO YOU SEE WHEN YOU LOOK AT ME?

BOYS ALWAYS BREAK THEIR PROMISES

Teddy Bears
Teddy Bears
Skating on
A frozen lake

Teddy Bears
Oh! Teddy Bears

Dancing on
A Snowflake

BEFORE THIS TIME ANOTHER YEAR

(GARE DE L'EST)
AMERICA'S DOG IS BOARDING THE 8PM TRAIN TO ANKARA

THAT DUDE IS BULLSHIT
MAL! NO!!
~CHANGE~

LOOKING FOR AMERICA'S DOG

AFTER MY GRANDPARENTS DIED, I NEVER SAW MY COUSINS, AUNTS OR UNCLES EVER AGAIN

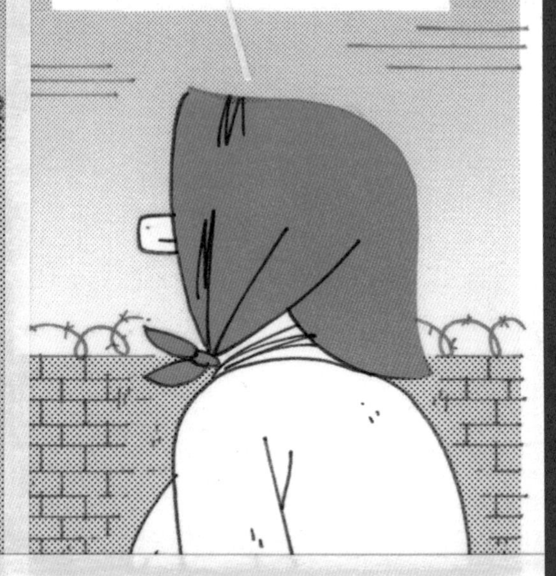
AFTER BURYING MY OWN PARENTS, I NEVER SAW MY SISTERS OR BROTHERS EVER AGAIN

AND AFTER MY HUSBAND DIED, I NEVER SAW MY CHILDREN EVER AGAIN
DA FUQ?

AFTER MY CAT DIED, I NEVER SAW MY DOG EVER AGAIN
BUT, HAVE YOU SEEN THIS DOG?

THIS IS HOW I DO IT NOW
I THINK AMERICA IS READY FOR MORE TOOTHPASTE-SAVING IDEAS

ONCE YOU'VE CUT OPEN THE TUBE + SCRAPED OUT ITS CONTENTS, YOU'RE STILL NOT DONE SAVING TOOTHPASTE
BRUSH
cres

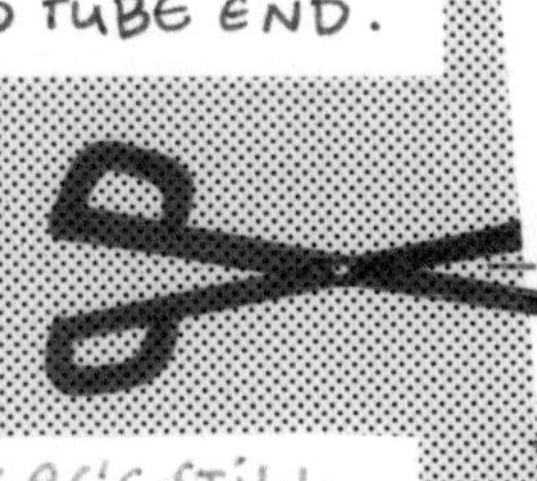
MAKE A SECOND CUT IN THE TUBE, LEAVING 1 1/2" BETWEEN CUT AND TUBE END.
cres
THERE'S STILL 1-2 BRUSHING'S WORTH OF PASTE IN THE NOZZLE

PLACE THE LARGE OPENING OVER YOUR MOUTH, FORMING A SEAL...
(REMOVE CAP)

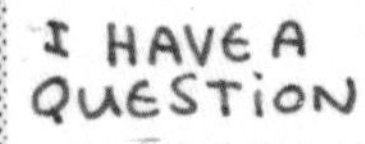
BLOW, CATCHING THE EXTRUDED PASTE ONTO THE BRISTLES OF YOUR BRUSH...
I HAVE A QUESTION

WOULDN'T IT BE NEATER AND EASIER TO BLOW THE PASTE INTO -RATHER THAN OUT OF- THE TUBE, THEN SCRAPE WITH A BRUSH AS BEFORE?
IT'S A FREE COUNTRY

WASHINGTON, D.C.

LOOKING FOR AMERICA'S DOG

BORNO

---BOKO HARAM WIVES---

AMERICA'S DOG IS GUARDING A DOZEN KIDNAPPED SCHOOLGIRLS

SAY WHAT?

LISTEN TO ME: THIS ANIMAL IS NOT BOKO HARAM...

IT'S THE WITCH

!?

GRRR

THROUGH HIS EYES I CAN SEE THE FACES OF HIS TRUE MASTERS

BE QUIET, YOU FOOL
YOU'LL GET US KILLED

I KNOW YOU CAN SEE ME, AMERICAN PRINCESS...

IF YOU WANT TO FIND YOUR DOG YOU MUST FIRST LOOK FOR US

LOOKING FOR AMERICA'S DOG

IF THEY FIND US OUT HERE, IT'S GOING TO BE UGLY...
WHO?
BOKO HARAM?
YES, BOKO HARAM

I SUPPOSE YOU THINK THE AMERICANS ARE LOOKING FOR US...
IF I DIDN'T, I NEVER WOULD HAVE RUN
SAME AS YOU
PF

BESIDES, THEY AREN'T LOOKING FOR US: THEY'RE LOOKING FOR THIS DOG

I DON'T BLAME THEM. HE LOOKS DELICIOUS

BOKO HARAM WIVES

IF YOU SHOOT YOUR FRIEND THEN YOU WILL HAVE US ALL TO YOURSELF...
?
!

IF YOU SHOOT YOURSELF THEN THIS DOG WILL TAKE YOU TO AMERICA WITH US
BANG

GOOD BOY
BANG
BANG

THIS DOG WILL CARRY YOU TO AMERICA IN HIS BELLY

TELEPATHIC COMMUNICATION

CALLING AMERICAN PRINCESS
COME IN, AMERICAN PRINCESS

HERE I AM
AND MY NAME IS SASHA
THAT'S FUNNY: MY NAME IS SASHA, TOO
OKAY, FINE

LISTEN, SASHA: CAN I TALK WITH YOU ABOUT BOYS?
BOYS? ME??
I MEAN, I GUESS SO
CRACK

I'M SO GLAD
LISTEN, SASHA...
I'MMA HAVE TO CALL YOU BACK

GET UP! SIS!
MY BAG!

GO NOW!
MAL!!
MY ZIPPER'S STUCK!

C'MON
FUCK!

FUCK!!

SASH!
HELP!!
?

YES-

LOOKING FOR AMERICA'S DOG

FOLLOW THE SOUTHERN CROSS UNTIL MORNING, THEN EAST TIL YOU FIND THE RIVER

ARE YOU NOT COMING WITH US?
OUR GUIDES ARE DEAD AND BOKO HARAM ARE EVERYWHERE

THOSE GUYS ARE LOSERS!
YOU, ALONE, HAVE NOBILITY OF PURPOSE

THAT GUY TURNED OUT TO BE PRETTY COOL

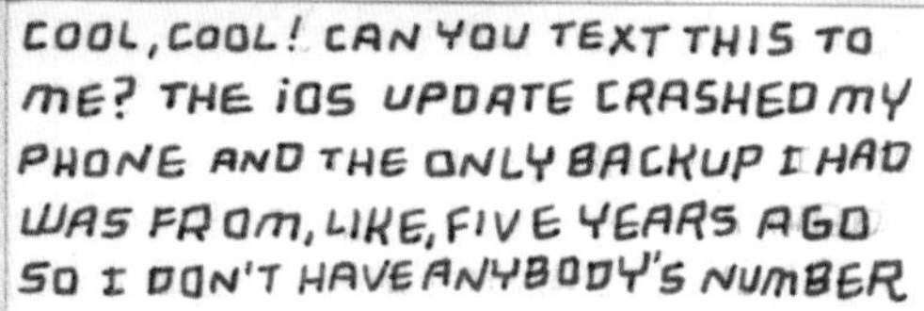

WASHINGTON, D.C.

LOOKING FOR AMERICA'S DOG

YOU REALLY CAN'T SEE BO ANYMORE?

NO

MY ESP HAS GONE AWAY

SO, WE'RE ON OUR OWN?

DON'T WORRY, MAL, THE SPIRIT TOLD US WHICH WAY TO GO

I DON'T SUPPOSE YOU CAN SEE WHAT DRAKE IS DOING RIGHT NOW, EITHER?
OH
I CAN GUESS!

DRAKE IS JERKING OFF IN THE SHOWER AGAIN

WHAT!? DOESN'T HE KNOW THERE'S A DROUGHT ON?

HE'S A DUMDUM

LOOKING FOR AMERICA'S DOG

WHO CARES, ANYWAY?

THIS WITCH HAS ... NERVE!

HEAVENLY FATHER... YOU ARE GRE

AND WE ARE GARBAGE... PLEASE

DON'T THROW ME AWAY

SHE TOLD US SOM

AMERICANS WO

RESCUE US FR

ATTACK, SISTERS! THEY

CANNOT KILL US ALL

AMERICA'S DOG

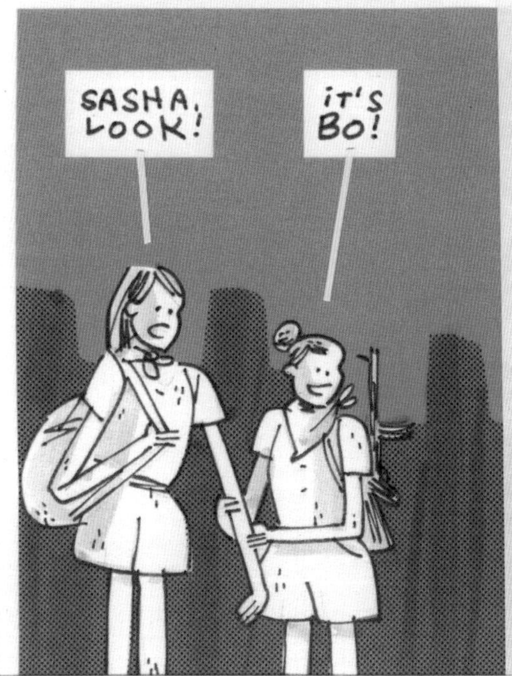

WHAT'S UP, LADIES
IN THE NAME OF GOD, WE CLAIM YOU AS BOKO HARAM WIVES
BRPP
BRP BRP

HEY GIRLS: EVERYBODY ATTACK THEM! THEY CAN'T POSSIBLY GET US ALL

WUT
YOU THREE FOLLOW ME
THE FUK
LET'S ROLL

THAT WAS BULLSHIT!
MAGIC
IT WAS MAGIC
BRPP
BRP
BRPP BRP
BRP
BRPPP
BRPP!

* AMERICA'S DOG *

BO
SQUEAK

OW!!
GROWFF

IT'S OK, BO...
IT'S OK...

A PAINLESS DEATH HOLDS NO MEANING

YOU'RE A WITCH! BRING OUR DOG BACK FROM THE DEAD
I DON'T HAVE A SPELL FOR THAT
THEN YOU SUCK...

MAYBE NOW YOU SEE WHAT IT'S LIKE FOR US HERE
NO ONE CARES WHAT IT'S LIKE FOR YOU HERE

YOUR SUFFERING IS INEVITABLE...

OURS INEXPLICABLE

UNITED STATES AFRICAN COMMAND
COMIN THRU
GET OUTTA THE WAY

YOU MAY NOT PASS
WUT!

SORRY, SASHA
YEAH

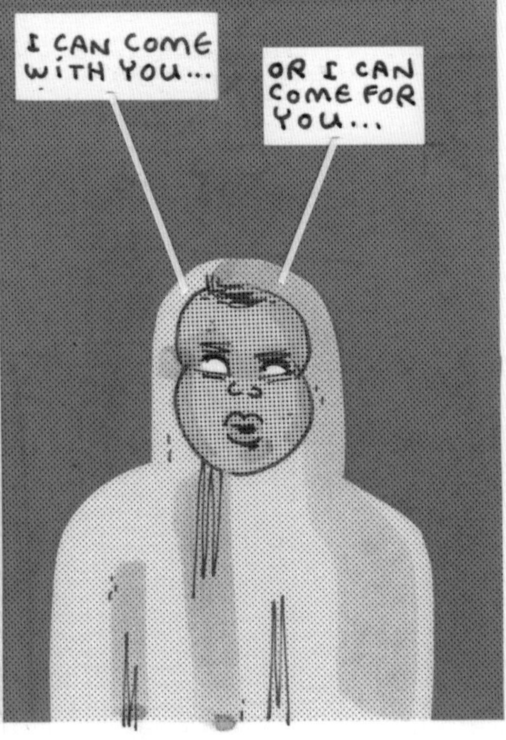
I CAN COME WITH YOU...
OR I CAN COME FOR YOU...

HILLARY RODHAM CLINTON

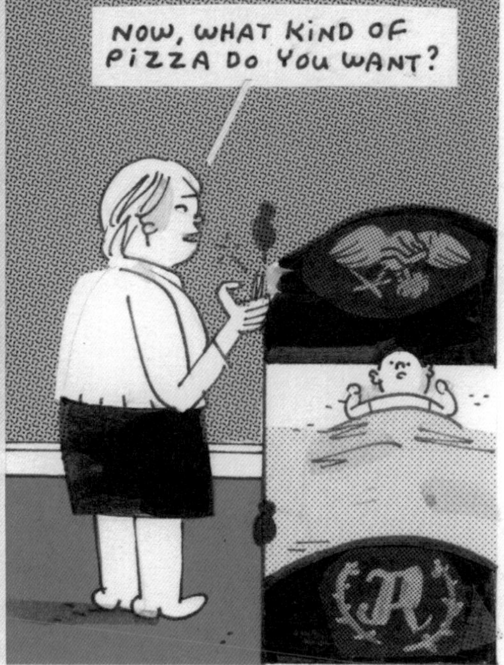

JOSEPH ROBINETTE BIDEN

SO, HE'S **NOT** RUNNING FOR PRESIDENT?

IT FIGURES! YOU KNOW HE OWES ME MONEY, RIGHT?

HUMBLE

WASHINGTON, D.C.

STEVE HARVEY MORNING SHOW

WEEKDAYS
6-10 AM

JOE BIDEN QUITS

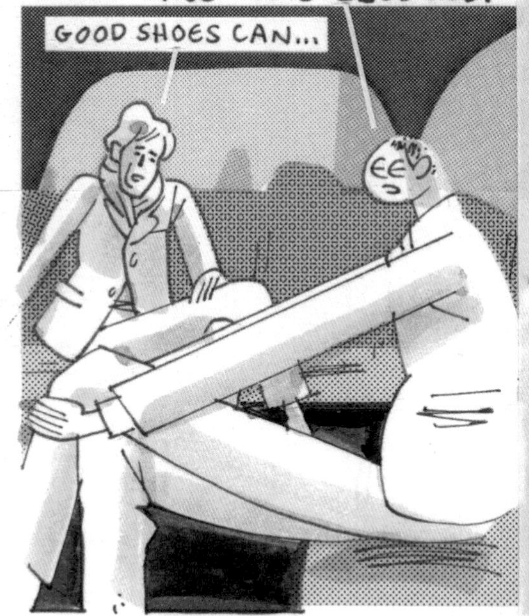

WASHINGTON, D.C.

I KNOW SOMEONE ELSE WHO'S GLAD TO SEE YOU, TOO...

ANDREWS AIR FORCE BASE

I GUESS YOU'RE AMERICA'S DOG NOW, SUNNY
SASH!

WHAT
DON'T LOOK AT ME LIKE THAT!
I MISS BO, TOO

I'M NOT MAD AT YOU, SASHA... IT'S JUST... MAYBE AMERICA DOESN'T NEED A DOG ANYMORE...
PAW

AT LEAST, NOT A BULLSHIT DOG LIKE SUNNY...

I WONDER, DARLING

FEED

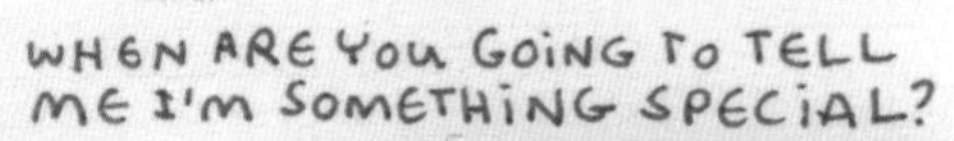
WHEN ARE YOU GOING TO TELL ME I'M SOMETHING SPECIAL?

Index

Fantagraphics Books 7563 Lake City Way NE Seattle, Washington 98115

Editorial Liaison: Gary Groth. Associate Publisher: Eric Reynolds. Publisher: Gary Groth. Production: Paul Baresh. Design Assistance: Jordan Crane and Michael Heck. Dedication: Charles and Charissa. First Fantagraphics edition: September, 2016. ISBN: 978-1-60699-955-4. Library of Congress Control Number: 2016950000. Printed in Korea.

STEVE

FUCKIN
RICH KIDS